P9-DVT-299

We Are Thankful

Written by Margaret McNamara
Illustrated by Mike Gordon

Ready-to-Read

Simon Spotlight
New York   London   Toronto   Sydney   New Delhi

SIMON SPOTLIGHT
An imprint of Simon & Schuster Children's Publishing Division
1230 Avenue of the Americas, New York, New York 10020
This Simon Spotlight edition September 2020
Text copyright © 2020 by Margaret McNamara
Illustrations copyright © 2020 by Mike Gordon
SIMON SPOTLIGHT, READY-TO-READ, and colophon are registered trademarks of
Simon & Schuster, Inc. For information about special discounts for bulk purchases,
please contact Simon & Schuster Special Sales at 1-866-506-1949
or business@simonandschuster.com.
Manufactured in the United States of America 0720 LAK
2 4 6 8 10 9 7 5 3 1
Cataloging-in-Publication Data for this title is available from the Library of Congress.
ISBN 978-1-5344-6825-2 (hc) • ISBN 978-1-5344-6824-5 (pbk)
ISBN 978-1-5344-6826-9 (eBook)

"Thanksgiving is coming soon," said Mrs. Connor.
"It is a time to think about what you are thankful for."

That night Reza sat down
with his mama.

They made a list of what
Reza was thankful for.

He was thankful for
his mama, his papa,
his brothers, his dog, snow,
his bike, and pumpkin pie.

"These are such good ideas!"
said his mama.

Reza was proud of his list.

At school the next day,
Mrs. Connor asked,
"What are you thankful for?"

Hannah's hand went up.

"I am thankful for my mom!"
said Hannah.

"I am thankful for my dad!"
said Ayanna.

"Oh no!" Reza thought.
"I have the same ideas
as everybody else!"

"I am thankful for my dog!"
said Michael.

"I am thankful for
my brothers and my bike!"
said Andrew.

Emma put up her hand.
"I am thankful for snow,"
said Emma, "and snow days."

Reza was so sad!
Almost all his good ideas
were taken!

The only one left was
pumpkin pie.

"Do you know what
I am thankful for?"
asked Nia.

"Fall leaves?" asked Reza.

"No!" said Nia.
"I am thankful for
pumpkin pie."

Now all Reza's good ideas
were gone.

"Reza," said Ms. Connor.
"What are you thankful for?"

Reza did not want to have
the same ideas as
everybody else.

Reza wanted to have a
new idea.
He thought and thought.

Then he smiled.

"I am thankful that
we have so much
to be thankful for,"
said Reza.

"Good idea!"
said Mrs. Connor.
"I am thankful for you all!"